by Teddy Slater
Illustrated by Sanja Rescek

ISBN 978-0-545-35181-2

12 11 10 9 8 7 6 5 4 3 14 15 16/0
Printed in the U.S.A. 40
First printing, September 2011

Hannah feels **happy**.
Hannah feels glad.

She's going to the park today—
just Hannah and her Dad.

Hannah feels **happy**.
Hannah feels **grand**.
Out on the sidewalk,
she takes her dad's hand.

Happiness lights up her face.
The park is Hannah's favorite place.

Hannah feels special.
Hannah feels **great**.
She skips ahead
right to the gate.

WOODLAND PARK

In front of the monkey bars,
Hannah sees May.
Poor May is having
an *un*-happy day.

"Hi!" Hannah hollers.
"I'm glad you're here, May.
Let's go on the seesaws.
They are right down this way."

When they get to the seesaws,
the two girls see Zack.

They give him big smiles,
and Zack smiles right back.

Outside the sandbox, they see their friend Tim.

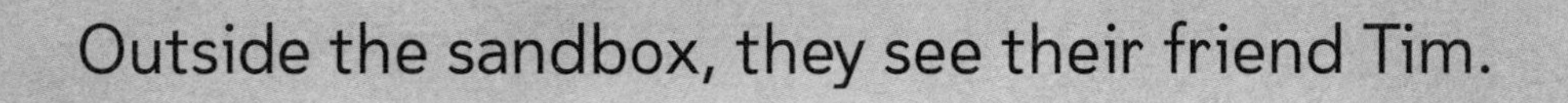

And now they share their joy with him.

Around and around, Hannah's happiness flows.
The more that she shares it, the more that it grows.

A Note for Parents

Communication is key.
As parents, we all want to see our children happy and to shield them from difficult and painful emotions. Unfortunately, that is not always possible. They are bound to experience a wide range of feelings: happiness and sadness, excitement and fear, and love and anger. It is possible, however, to help our children deal with their unhappy feelings so they can fully enjoy the happy ones. We may often have some practical advice to offer, but the most successful way to help a child cope with difficult feelings is to keep the lines of communication open.

Talking about their feelings to a concerned and empathetic parent teaches children that it is normal to feel sad, angry, or scared sometimes. Equally important, it allows them to express and explore these feelings while giving you the opportunity to offer comfort and support. Trusting you to understand, they will learn to trust their own ability to handle troubling emotions and to feel safe and secure in the world.

HANNAH FEELS HAPPY
In this book, Hannah feels happy when she and her father share some special time together at the park. Basking in her father's love and attention, she radiates joy. Throughout the day, that joy rubs off on everyone she meets.

Children may find fleeting pleasure in a new toy, a special treat, or a favorite activity. But those who know they are loved experience deep and lasting happiness. They, in turn, become loving and sensitive to the feelings of others and are able to fully enjoy the world and people around them.